Dies Natalis Solis Invicti

Sunrise in the Shadow of My Soul

Angela F. Wheeler

Dies Natalis Solis Invicti:
Sunrise in the Shadow of My Soul

Published By Fox Creative Works, LLC

ISBN 978-0-578-01340-4

Printed and bound in the United States of America

FORWARD

"Dies Natalis Solis Invicti" chronicles what could be any woman's journey in search of her own inner light. When you're lost and alone, misunderstood and ridiculed, and continuously neglected and admonished, the world around you can become cold and harsh. Loneliness seems to find you even in the most crowded of places, even in the holiest of places. Left to these conditions long enough, even the most resilient of Spirits begins to fade.

In her effort to survive, she calls out to the one power who can act on her behalf. As she reaches her lowest point, and her spirit begins to fade, and the abyss threatens to consume her very soul, the painful prayers that she sent up, returned to her, answered in a way she had not anticipated.

From unknown regions, he entered her life. Unassuming, friendly and caring he warms the cold regions of her soul. As time passes, his unassuming demeanor takes on a regal persona, his friendly nature transforms to a loving embrace, and his care taker stance takes on the transfixed position as her ever loving protector. Before her very eyes and in her warming heart, the answered prayer *that entered her life as an unassuming figure transformed into what has become the light of her life; He has, in time, become her "Unconquered Sun".*

Join her journey as she follows her spiritual guide back from the abyss and once again finds her "way" in life, understanding that in the end Love not only restores one's life, but rekindles one's Spirit, as she continues on her own journey to become "An Unconquered Sun".

Dedication

To "My Eternal Sun",
Always, All Ways...

Table Of Contents

The Beginning

Sunrise

He walks into my life
like the sun rising in the morning

Shining light and warmth on my dark soul.

My soul which once burned brightly but is
now cold embers

With a word the embers spark
and with a touch the flames ignite

Our souls entwined
we burn bright like twin suns.

Passion's Flames

You are beautiful...
a timeless beauty like an angel in
all his fearsome power

Do I dare touch you?

My mortal flesh may burn from your
shining glory.

But even so,

Let me lay in your arms till I am consumed
by your love's passionate fire.

An Answered Prayer

I called out into the void...

and you answered...

Thank you for filling my heart.

Hera and Zeus
(To Kiss the Sky)

I am mother earth......

Ageless......

You are father sky...

Timeless.....

Constantly caressing me....
And protecting me....

Our union forged before the dawn of man.

Ageless.......
Timeless.....
Endless.......

Confessions
(of a Conquered Queen)

They call me a queen, some dare say goddess

Men worship at my feet and wait for the merest smile

But before you I am powerless

I wait with baited breath for you to call me; count the minutes until I can see you... I tremble in anticipation of your touch - to worship at your feet and wait for your smile

The radiant beauty of God shines forth from your soul

You are my King

Promises, Promises

Spoken promises bind our love through the good times and bad...

Unspoken promises bind us to grow together in love and wisdom...But that was when I thought you were the sun and I grew towards you...

But soon I began to wither and die... and there were no tears of sorrow to mourn my passing. Now the true sun has risen in my life and I flourish once again. I grow towards the light as it revolves around me and I grow straight and tall.

His drops of laughter nourish me like rain. The spoken promises begin to bind my roots and branches...

I long to be free to reach out to the sun.

No more promises...
No more promises...
Only love

In Search of An Answer

I don't know what I am searching for, but I know I must walk towards the mountain.

I am drawn to that mountain like Moses, to hear a word from the Lord

I pray that before my life's end, my soul will find what it is longing for...

It is beyond this physical plane, and more than my mind can conceive...

So I continue my walk towards the mountain,

where I'll pray for a word from the Lord.

Gentle Whispers

Soft candlelight and caresses....

Whispered "I love you's" in passion's warm afterglow.

I could stay like this forever, never reaching morning...just basking in the warmth of you, my own sun.

Your smile caresses my soul like the sun caresses my cheek.

Does the sun love me?
I don't know...

For now it's enough for me to stay in the soft candlelight and whisper "I Love You", in the warmth of my sun.

Just Words

Love you

Care for you

Found each other

Words

Just words

Words seemingly so casually tossed about
like bread crumbs lead the naive sparrow
right to the wolf's lair.

An Unreality

In the dark I pretend you are my one true love

I whisper "I love you" but it is not meant for your ears

You are a fantasy, not reality

You are a remembrance of what my love used to be and a broken dream of what my love should be

And so I count the days until I can return to my one true love and reality

The Fox & The Wolf

Am I the innocent lamb seduced by the wolf?

Or am I the sly fox that tricks the dove into her lair?

Perhaps we are both predators – at odds in the deadly game of love.

Will I survive? I still suffer from my last battle and I fear this new opponent will deliver the fatal blow.

Why don't I end this game before it is too late? Because underneath the sly fox is an innocent lamb that cannot resist the ravenous wolf....

Look out

Because the sly fox may just survive

"The One" in A Million

I have loved a million women and I tell you
I will love a million more

Will I love another like you?

No, our minds and souls like one

Our bodies eagerly learn more of each other

No I will not love another the way I love
you but I've got to keep searching

Only a million more to go

From Fantasy to Reality

(A Quantum Leap)

From fantasy to reality, the line is blurred.

You are my dream but now in my life

I dream of your touch and then you touch
me

I imagine what you will say and you
whisper in my ear

Day and night, hearing you in my mind and
now in my life

My fantasy has become my reality

Manifestation
"In The Beginning"

I cannot keep my heart from loving you;

You know I have loved you from the beginning.

I formed you in my mind and spoke you into existence

Now with every word the creation shapes the creator

And I cannot keep my heart from loving you.

You know I have loved you since my beginning.

Dreams Unfulfilled

I cry because I cannot find the man of my dreams... I found in reality someone that was almost.

But now I know that almost does not fulfill a dream.

I cry because I found the man of my dreams. I found in reality someone that belongs to another. And now I know that he cannot fulfill my dreams.

I cry because I could not have the man of my dreams... I found that in reality dreams cannot be fulfilled.

From My Dreams to Reality

If I somehow obtain my dream, will I be able to keep it?

Or will it vanish under the bright light of day?

It is a thin veil of hope that covers the truth my heart does not want to see.

Sometimes I allow myself to believe he is mine. My mind knows what my heart denies and for a moment I falter.

The light of truth quickly burns away the vapors of deception like the morning dew.

I cannot hold onto this dream...

I am only left with truth.

Convergence
(When Souls Collide)

What we are experiencing is a convergence
of mind, body, and soul.

Beyond words, beyond promises...

It is and shall always be...

called love

A Soul Constrained

Chains that bind you

Chains that bind me made from cruel hope

Hope tells me to stay one more day. Hope tells me to find some way to work it out because it will get better.

Hope makes me try desperately. What can break the cruel chains of hope?

Nothing.... Even when life has beaten and broken me.... There is still hope.

So here I'll stay and hope that one day we will both be free.

What I Believe

I don't believe in love everlasting...

Love that lasts beyond our mortal bodies
        But how do I explain you?

You reached out and in a flash our souls touched. And I feel complete even when we are apart.

But I won't call it love... because I don't believe in love everlasting -

Love that lasts beyond our mortal bodies

        So how do I explain you?

                Soul mate

The Spark of Life

My heart sings and my soul dances with joy.

I am light
I am love

Come dance with me, my love
join your light with mine

Let us form a universe as our energies merge
and explode in ecstasy

We are light
We are love
We are one

Understanding

Our souls called out to each other as our
minds struggled to understand why we were
drawn to each other

As we grew to understand the bond between
us our bodies joined the dance of heart and
mind

Now,

We are one

In Remembrance of Love

Here, away from the cares of the world I remember why I once loved you...

And I love you again.

Here, in your arms, I remember how I used to love you....

And I love you again.

I remember it was always you...

And again I love you.

If We Care

Let us part now while we still care for each other...

Before the cold wind of reality cools our burning desires...

And lifts the veil of love's first bloom from our mind's eye.

Let us part now, so I can remember you fondly

And not embarrassment that turns to anger

Before the morning sun sheds its light on our dark deeds

And reveals to the world our lies

Let us part now, if we care for each other

Fool's Gold

So they think the newness of our love will gently fade like the shine on a cheap gold ring...

Don't they understand?

Our love is like gold purified in the fiery furnace of heartache and lost chances.

It is pure and will not fade.

Eating From The Tree of Knowledge

I long for someone to love me as I love him,
as deeply, as completely....

To give over himself and allow me into the
dark chambers of his heart, mind, and soul

I would say that I never found a man to
confess his love, to express his love in terms
of eternal, soul mate, or fate but there was
one...

I know now that he did not lie and I broke
his heart

I am perhaps the biggest liar of all for until
now I have never loved a man completely
and let him into the dark chambers of my
heart, mind, and soul -

and now it is my heart that is broken.

Shadows of A Dream

This started as tendrils of dreams that
slowly twisted and combined
until it had a life of its own.

We love each other and look for us.

But life moves on as the sun rises every
morning and dreams slowly unravel and
fade away.

By morning us will be gone without even a
memory of our love.

Can You Keep A Secret?

I'm a secret so I am not a friend because that would imply visible dependability

I'm not a secret so I am not the other woman because that would imply some softly spoken commitment of love.

Can there be friendship and love without dependability and commitment?

Are we really just two people who happen to be traveling along the same road at the same time?

If so; then when it is time to choose which fork to take there will be nothing to compel me or you to continue the journey together?

That is a privilege reserved only for friends and lovers.

The King's Seal

I try to keep my focus on the physical but again my body betrays me.

And with each touch the bond of mind and heart grow stronger...

Let this be the last time we touch and pray it is not the final seal on my heart.

The Long And Lonely Road

I choose to walk this path with you, how
could I know it would be so lonely?

I found another to walk with and though he
told me I could not, I tried...

And so I find myself alone again but without
even silence to keep me company.

The Fool that Follows the Fool

Didn't your grandmother say "Don't let the little boys fool you?"

You know I didn't mean for you to love me....

You know I used your own words to weave my spell.

It's always been about the physical - don't be confused.

My attention is only to fuel the flames. And the fun is in the chase.

Well, I've caught you now and I grow bored.

No, don't say you love me - you just sound like a fool.

Ideal Love?

I don't think I am in love with you....

I think I am in love with the idea of you...

Just a diversion to keep my mind off of my reality...

a distraction from the mundane.

And when you're gone, what will be my next obsession?

The Flower

I was a delicate flower withering on the
path but the warmth of your love,
my sun, renewed me.

Your gentle touch supported me and your
drops of kindness restored me.

Does a flower love the sun and rain and the
gentle breeze?

I don't know... but this delicate flower needs
your light and kindness to continue.

The Stand

Here I stand, outside your life....

Wishing it was me that had your pledge of devotion and unending love...

Hale-Bopp

Like a comet from the vast expanse of space
you come near my world...

Your beauty dazzles me and for a moment
you are more beautiful than my own sun.

I want to follow you...but it would mean
death to leave my sun for though you burn
bright you cannot sustain me.

So I continue in my pre-ordained orbit
and you will soon pass me by and I am
grateful once again for my own sun.

Gone But Not Forgotten

Morning is coming and the dream of us is
slowly unraveling and fading away.

I said that by morning us would be gone
without even a memory of our love...

But that is not true - for just like a
nightmare - this dream can shape my
waking hours.

I will mourn the passing of us barely formed
and hold its beauty in my heart.

The Breakthrough

The Haunting of Your Heart

I'm not in love with you anymore but you refuse to let me go.

And I am like a ghost that you keep tethered to your world.

I haunt the rooms, no warmth, just a cold chill and gnashing teeth.

Can't you see there is no fire in my eyes? Or are you waiting to see the fires of hell?

Let me go, let me move to the other side so I can live again.

The Request

I am almost free...

And I see you and through you. You try to hide your true nature and feelings but you are more transparent than you know.

I see kindness and love and a spirit that struggles to be free. A spirit weighed down by the cares of this world.

Free your spirit, go with me and let us create our own world.

Go with me, I am almost free...

The Un-Extraordinary Queen

Look at this Queen, so regal. See how she shines, her beauty and intellect are daunting.

So many want her, want to possess her, want to be her - to be special.

How sad, to see this Queen, her shine fading - the regal façade, the illusion broken

When she realizes she is just like us - she just wants to be special

Growing Up

I try to be mature, a grownup but I feel like such a little girl. I'm afraid to make the tough decisions and take the next step.

But just like a child takes a step back to the comfort zone before moving forward, I must take a step back.

I embrace the little girl in me and together we will take the next step.

Look at me; I'm all grownup...

Mariah

I am the wind and I cannot be contained…

My soft caress can soothe your fevered brow
Or I can fan the flames of passion

I love you and then I'm gone but always near

You can't contain me
I am the wind.

Mariah II

I am the wind and I cannot be contained

My gentle touch caresses your cheek and soothes your soul

I fuel the fire that burns in your heart and loins

You know I can support and lift you to heights unknown

Feel me but you can't keep me for I am the wind

And I cannot be contained

You Are The Wind

You are the wind, it is true; and you cannot be contained but I am the water and it is I who gives you strength

I stir you to heights of passion and it is I who calms you down.

I am the water,

And I am your inspiration.

The Flower

My spirit once completely tied down by
earthy cares is almost free

I have glimpsed through the barrier to see
God and He has touched me

Just a few more ties to break and I will be
free to pass through the barrier

I will see God

No Promises

I thought there could be no promises because
you are not free

But I was wrong, you are free

Free to choose to love me while I am here

And because I am free, I can't promise to
stay as long as you love me

So, no promises because we are both free

Matters of the Heart

I accept my role in the breaking of my heart. Too quickly I gave my heart to you when you barely touched my soul, mind, or body.

I thought we could grow together, instead we grew apart.

Leaving me alone and my heart shattered.

In my loneliness my heart is healing. Next time I give my heart only to him that completely touches my soul, mind, and body.

Oh Well

I'm not in love with you anymore

But I don't have anything else so I'll stay

See Ya

I don't love you anymore. And I don't have to ask you to let me go.

My heart is free, no longer bound to you to be misused and uncared for...

My heart is free to find comfort and protection in another's arms.

Free to express passion and joy – to feel the warmth of the sun.

My heart is free and I am already gone.

Nightmare

I was asleep, caught in a nightmare. Day after day the same torture.

Suddenly a light appeared on the horizon. My sun, so brilliant and beautiful rose in my life.

His light and love awakened me

Day after day I am bathed in his love and living out my dreams.

Quietly Fade to Black

My light is faltering, and I am starved for love - I should say goodbye.

I wonder will you notice I'm gone, if I don't say goodbye? With your world so full of love and light, will my little spark going out make a difference?

And if I do say goodbye? Could you spare a little more of your love to fuel my dying soul?

Even so, I would not drain that beautiful spirit and deny the world. But I don't have the strength to utter those final words that would block your love and light. So I'll just fade out quietly and I won't say goodbye....

The Truth

I must face the truth you have already seen,
this must end - it has ended.

It doesn't matter if you love me, or loved me;
your life is closed to me. Why do I hover at
your door waiting to come in? Love?

It doesn't matter if I love, I must move on
but not in search of another door to open.
Perhaps that is the real truth I don't want to
face.

Rediscovery

I thought I didn't love you anymore and then I found her.

But as I thought of my new love I found that my love was you.

Her laughter, her countenance, all reminded me of why I love you.

I know I don't love her anymore because I found the love I had for you.

Liar, Liar

We lie to ourselves everyday. Like I am lying to myself when I say I don't love you deeply. I want to say I just want you to worship and adore me. I want to say when I grow bored of your attentions or I find someone who amuses me more I will let you go.

You lie to yourself and say that I put some spell on you. What am I? A voodoo Queen or goddess that controls your will?

We lie to ourselves everyday, what other lies have you told yourself?

My Happy Place

When I think of my love I feel contentment and peace.

I feel like I can weather any storm and I have such happiness I can stand almost anything - even staying with you seems like a possibility because the storm isn't so bad anymore.

My love gives me such contentment and peace.

And I Will Always Love You

I will always love you. How do I know this?

Because we are parting before we hurt each other... before words cause pain and life causes us to drift apart. Before the haze of love that clouded our eyes clears and you see the real me.

We part while we can blame circumstance and hate as the reason. While your kisses make me faint with desire and your strong touch sends waves of ecstasy through my body.

I will always hold your love as the most pure and the most passionate. All other loves will pale in comparison and I will always love you.

Dawn

I wait in darkness for my sun is not with me. I look forward to morning, when my sun returns to me.

In the darkness, I remember his face, the sound of his laughter, and his sweet caress.

I remember, but it is not enough. I want to see his light as he gazes upon my beauty. I long to feel my sun's warmth as he gently caresses my body.

I can barely restrain my eagerness to receive his sweet sun drops in our ecstasy. I want to be with my sun until completion.

I wait in darkness for morning is coming and with it, my precious sun.

Eden I

I am immersed in my love, and it is Paradise. I couldn't bear to leave it. Your warmth and light give strength to my soul. Your sweet caress soothes my restless spirit.

It is the serpent that makes me doubt your love and brings the risk of expulsion. Can a mere mortal stand to leave Paradise?

No more questions, just let me find myself in your warm embrace, surrounded by your love.

Let me cradle you in my valley as we rise to new heights of ecstasy.

Here immersed in my love, in Paradise.

Duet

Two minds connect

Two hearts unite

Two souls touch

Bodies intertwined

A spark
A new life begins

Surrender

My love, my sun, come to me now and bathe me in your warmth.

Caress me with your light.

When I gaze upon your beauty I forget to breathe, all time is frozen.

Each touch from you makes me burn with desire. Your smoldering eyes sear my heart and brands it as your own.

I open myself to you completely and your magnificence consumes me. When I am in your arms all cares are burned away. Your essence fills me, our bodies cannot contain our spirits and we fly to the stars.

Come to me now my love, come with me...

Solar Circuit

I cannot rush the sun; he will come at his own time.

I wait with much impatience for my sun to rise. I know he must shine on others; he is too precious, too bountiful for one mere mortal. Still, I say come to me now my sun, leave the others and stay with me.

Bathe me in your eternal light, consume me with your passion until I burn like a star.

I cannot rush the sun but let his time be now.

Thoughts From "The Sun" to "The One"

The sun warms the heart, nourishes the soul and brings life to the dormant valleys of one's essence.

The sun's expression of what it thinks of "The One" it warms in its glow is far deeper than the casual definition of the word LOVE.

Render Unto Caesar

I am "The One"
Give me your mind - all light and even the darkest corners - I can survive

I am "The One"
Give me your heart, cold as ice or hot as the sun - I will embrace it and care for it as my own.

I am "The One"
Give me your body - full of primal sexuality and virility - I will take all of you

I am "The One"
Give me your soul and let us journey to heaven

I am "The One"

Who Am I?

I am "The One"....

The one that brings order to chaos....

The one that inspires.....

The one for whom the sun shines

Ambition

I am fulfilling my destiny to become a goddess. I am bathed in power – filled with power.

My spirit fights to see beyond the confines of my flesh – the boundaries that limit my power to the here and now, to the realm of mortals.

I must go beyond the fear in my heart and move to the next level.

I have the power to shape my world and have my heart's desire.

I can even dare reach for the sun.

Lo, I Stand At The Door and Knock

Once again I am left standing outside....
My love for you burns like the sun and I
cannot quench it nor hide it.

You have professed your love for me yet it seems so easy for you to set me aside.

What secrets do you keep, secrets that seem to cool your desire for me?

Are you afraid my love will suffocate in the dark recesses of your mind?

Try me, for I cannot love you truly if I do not know you truly.

Trust my love and let me in....

E Pluribus Unum

My sun is so close, so bright.
At first the light is so bright, I seem to be on
fire – I am brilliant, beautiful. I am the one.

In the course of time, as it is with all
heavenly bodies, the sun moves away....

It's daylight.... And all is revealed in the
true light of day.

My physical imperfections, the darkest
corners of my mind and heart are exposed.

Am I still the one? Or one out of many?

Let Me

The light was slowly fading... too late I
realize I'm losing the sunlight.

I cried out into the void but you were gone,
only the cold darkness,
nothing to light my way

Open your eyes and see me....

I am sunlight; let me light your way

Call out into the void and I will answer

Let me be your sun

The Haunting of My Heart

You haunt me....

Always lurking in the back of my mind even when I don't realize it...Coloring my thoughts, words, and deeds with feelings of inadequacy and failure.

Failure to love you enough or inadequate to meet your needs...

How much more should I have given? What more could I have done?

Despite my logical reasoning of the facts, my heart sill drives - I must banish your ghost or I will always fear my ideal man will find me less than his ideal woman

There I said it.... So perhaps this relationship will not end the same way

Damn, here's another ghost

Mistake

I didn't mean for this to happen

I have become what I always despise.

A woman weak willed and waiting for her
lover to spare a few drops of affection

Caring what he thinks of her, caring how he
likes her to look...

Submitting to his will

But this feels right, my place is at his side -
supporting him in his endeavors,
encouraging him, loving him

The woman I have become...

The other woman is to be pitied - she just
needed to love the right man

I Miss You

You said I shouldn't miss you, but I do...

I fill every waking hour with life and work,
but at night I am alone with my thoughts.

Sometimes I chose to be alone and sometimes
I am lonely; And that is when your memory
is strongest and I want to reach out to you...

Into your life...

You said I shouldn't miss you, but I think
you miss me too.

Dreamchaser

When do you stop chasing a dream?

I dreamed a dream of a man

Regal bearing, kind hearted, full of
knowledge, light of spirit and loving

I dreamed a dream of a man, who could
touch my soul,

who could be an anchor and a guide

I dreamed a dream of a man

But when do you stop chasing a dream?

Alpha

I am Alpha
I knew from the beginning you were not...
Oh, you think you are with your high
powered job, big car, and money

But when it's gone, how do you measure
your worth?

You want me to be submissive but I cannot,
not for you - only for an Alpha

Hey, at least I let you live

Don't Move

If I squint my left eye and turn my head
slightly to the right then I can almost
pretend you're not there

No, don't say a word and don't move

I want to forget you are here; I need some
time to myself, for myself

I need to think about where I've been, where
I am, and where I want to go

Maybe you should do the same.... Then you
would see we haven't been together for a
long time

Then you would really go and I wouldn't
have to pretend anymore

Maybe if I squint both eyes...?

Dreamchaser II

When do you stop chasing a dream?

You always wanted to be your own boss, or
a dancer, or singer, or a million other
possibilities

Life gets in the way

So when do you stop chasing a dream?

Children, educational issues, job, friends,
money, health - life

So when do you stop chasing a dream?

Never

You just dream a new dream

Clarity

I wish I could say I'm confused but I'm not. I am very clear in my feelings for you.

Sadness:
For the life you let slip through your fingers

Anger:
Because you let your pride dictate your actions regardless of the consequences

Loneliness:
Because you can no longer even be a shadow of my dream man

Yes, my feelings are clear

Painfully so….

Matters of the Heart II

I envy those with a practical view of life for though I am ruled by logic my heart is the driver.

Despite all calculated results I still hold out for the romantic and happy ending. I have hope that my ideal man, my dream will come and take his rightful place in my life.

That one special man every girl dreams of – her prince, no her King will stride in victoriously and take her.

With all the evidence laid before me, my heart can't, won't let go. Always hoping for just one more minute of you, like I'm trying to store up your light for my dark days when you are gone, when the practicalities of life draw you away...

It is then I will hold you only in my heart.

Who Was The One?

Who answered my prayer, my plea, and my siren's song?

My prayer for someone to understand my particular brand of crazy, my view of the universe.

My plea that my spirit not wither and die, someone to talk to, who appreciates my intellect.

My siren's song, someone to appreciate my beauty, inside and out.

When I was in darkness I called out into the void and you appeared; now I am become light

The answer to my prayer, my plea... is you.

Light

You have brought a light to my life that had not been seen in years.

You rekindled my light and now I am become light.

Light Rediscovered

Like a comet from the vast expanse of space
you come near....

But you are more than a comet made of cold
rock - you are a sun bringing light and love
into my life

Your tendrils of love re-ignite the cold
embers of my heart

Now I have a new dance, a new orbit that
joins with yours.

Twin suns bringing light and love to so
many worlds.

Love's Rapture

Come with me my love...

Let us talk till midnight and dance until dawn

Watching the sunrise in each other's embrace

We'll commune with nature and unravel the mysteries of the universe

We'll explore our souls and find God

Come with me my love...

Come...

Is This Love?

How can you profess love for me when you do not support my dreams? I have a fire burning inside that cannot be contained.

But instead of helping me channel it safely - you drown it with no support and pessimistic sayings.

Embarrassed rather than joyful of my creative works... You say you have no imagination - maybe that's why you can't dream.

So you'll always be the destroyer, the dark that tries to blot out my light.

No love at all.

I Know Who You Are

You tell me you are not the man I think you are... Being a dreamer and in need of a dream fulfilled perhaps I only saw you through my mind's eye.

Having a giving heart and in need of love perhaps I grasped for your heart too soon.

Having a free spirit and a need for a kindred soul perhaps I wandered too far.

So if you are not the man I think you are, perhaps you are the man yet to be....

The Question

To answer the question would I every marry again.... Right now the answer is "I don't know".

I never imagined I would really meet a man that was a kindred spirit, regal bearing, and a gentle spirit.

I never thought I would meet a man that connected with me mentally, spiritually, and physically.

If ever I meet another man like this perhaps then I would bind myself to him knowing I would still be free.

Freedom

My spirit is not truly free for I can only
imagine how it would feel to be fully free of
gravity.

All the things that weigh me down, keep me
chained to the mundane.

I don't wish for fame and fortune or
greatness, I just want to live this
extraordinary life I have been given

To love freely, truly, unselfishly, not
hoarding it in fear for later days.

I know when I let go of my shackles,
jealousy, envy, hate, me, me, and all mine

I will be free

I will fly

A Woman's Love

How does a woman love? Is it with calculated winks and glances or shy peeps? Does she have sweet laughter or giggle fits at his slightest antic?

Does she give sultry looks or blush at his touch?

A woman loves in all these ways for she is innocent and worldly at the same time. An angel and a sinner.

And you love them both

What Is Left?

Is there nothing left but bitterness and anger?

Do you have no kind words? No warm touch?

I begged you to let go while there was yet some haze of love left... but you refused. Now you have nothing for me but cold heartless anger and vengeance.

Vengeance that will surely kill you before me for I have retrieved my heart and cannot be touched.

So you are left with bitterness and anger, and no one to care.

As The Sun Rises

As the sun rises

My path is lit that was only in darkness

As the sun rises

My soul is warmed that was growing cold

As the sun rises

The Calling

My sun is hot and I am burning with desire
His warm touch and sensuous kisses make
me want to bear my soul

His passionate embrace ignites my very
being and I am aflame

Your smoldering eyes liquefy me... the cares
of this world are not enough to quench my
desire

Come to me my love and illuminate me from
within, burn your essence on my soul

Let me be sun kissed, leave your mark on me
so the world will know you are my Sun King
and I am Your Queen

Speak To Me

Say it, say the words in the cold light of day.
The words you whispered so sweetly to me
after I gave myself to you.

Tell me if our passion is lust mindlessly
fueled by our bodies or tell me our passion is
love fueled by our mind and soul

Tell me...

Say the words in the cold light of day, say it
sweetly or whisper it softly

Just say the words

Dreams

Morning is here and I finally hear you... you talked to me all night but you know I'm a dreamer

Dreamers can't stop and I've lived in this world for so long it's hard to see reality

The sun may come in the morning but it is nighttime when the sun is mine and mine alone.

So go if you must, I will always have you in my dreams.

Questions

Why so many questions?

Because I cannot see through your eyes....

Why you love...
How you love...
Imperfection and doubt

You are the Sun King and I am but a humble peasant grateful for the splendor of your beautiful countenance to shine upon me. I bask in your warmth and at the same time am in awe of your magnificence.

I want to see myself as you see me, as your Queen.

The Creator

I am your creation
Images from your imagination
Beams of light from your radiant soul
Formed by your hands
Brought to life by your will and with a will

With a will to choose
I choose to love
I am your creation, formed in love and
bathed in love, giving love to my creator

Dichotomy

Innocent and worldly

Exposed to the ways of the world yet you remain pure of heart

The beauty of your soul shines forth for all to see

How can I not desire to be in your presence?

Saint and Sinner
Sinner and Saint

The Moon

As the sun rises in my life I realize I had been following the moon on a clear cold starry night.

Frostbitten and dying the sun's rays warm me and bring me back to life

Now I live in the sun never to be fooled by the moon again

Just In Time

Once too late I realized who truly loved me
and how I had broken his heart

Now I see one that loves me mind, spirit,
and body

Once I realized in time who truly loves me
and I will not break his heart

The Cinderella Story

I am a Queen, but I will always need my Sun King, for without him I am but a humble peasant wasting away in the darkness.

He nourishes and restores me, he is my support.

My sun draws his strength from the creator and as was ordained he guides me in His path.

I sit at his feet in awe of his beauty and marvel that he has chosen to be my King, my Sun King.

And to make me his Queen...

The Better Way

Better to die lonely and alone than to be tethered and die lonely in the midst of cold silence.

At least alone I would have my dreams to accompany me.

Let my heart be silent in this matter, for it wants to wait for him to come to me... my mind knows the truth, no one knows the future and I must live while I can.

The way he touches me, I know there will never be another and I will settle for no less – not again, never again.

If ever he comes to me I will accept him and if not, then I die alone with my dreams.

And in the end isn't that how it must be with us all?

Let Love Release Me

Your reaction confirms my worst fear. You never loved me.... How could you move from love to hate in 60 seconds? Anger I understand, but there was never hate.

Even now,

There is sorrow and sadness but no energy for hate, only for living. You are the walking dead for as sure as you were born your hate has killed you.

No love   no joy

Just speculation and counter moves to what you think will be a hateful move.

If I am wrong, if you ever loved me, then find it now and wish me well

And live

Just My Imagination

Do you know how I have longed for a kindred spirit, someone to tell my secrets, share my fantasies, talk to me, support me, and adore me?

You came like rain in a drought, restoring my dying soul - a light in the darkness of my soul.

No poetry with eloquence and dramatic effect could demonstrate what you mean to me.

Life before you was only in my imagination and now I am living.

Just A Token

Accept this token of my affection to hold
until I can hold you in my arms forever.

Look at it and think of me hoping I will
return.

And should the unthinkable happen know
that I wanted to return, to come back to you
my love, my true love.

It's only a token but it represents the love for
you I hold in my heart.

Family Dinner

Must I sit through another big family dinner? Why try to hide what's not in our hearts? Isn't that why we're in the mess we are now? Keeping secrets, pretending the family was what it isn't?

Should've left long ago and now I'm trapped. Trying to make the best of it while held within the boundaries of appearances.

How to move on with my life and keep the charade? Condemning myself to loneliness in the midst of a crowd. Denying myself the warmth of the sun. The sun I've waited so long to find and he may never come again.

I'm thinking about my sun and they think my smiles are for them... hey, at least it gets me through dinner. Maybe I can get some sun drops for dessert?

The Realization

I sit at the table watching all the slumped shoulders signifying "I'm beaten" "I give up".

While I sit head up and shoulders back. After all, don't I profess to have the backing of the One True God?

With Him I can overcome any obstacle, remove any mountain, and have my heart's desire. If I say He walks with me, surrounds me, and moves me.... Then I need to show the world. A journey starts not with a single step, but a thought - I can, I will.

Order My Steps

I need order in my life lest I fly away. I must label you, to categorize you lest I become consumed in you and lose my way. I feel myself pulled in so many directions I need a light to keep me on the path.

But you must move with me, you cannot stand still for I will leave you. I cannot stop for it would be the death of me.

You are my sun, my light, and my guide. I will follow you all ways, always, if it be your will.

If it be your will, I will fly to you my sun

Mother Earth

Mother Earth revolves around the sun.

Without him she would be cold and barren.

Alone in the void.

The Awakening

I am awakening... once trapped in an endless nightmare I begin to see my reality.

I am beautiful, intelligent, warm, and compassionate.

Who has awakened me? It is the rising of the sun.

In Your Arms

I want to stay here in your arms forever my sun; your warmth caresses so tenderly.

Your laughter sparkles in your eyes like dewdrops in the breaking dawn.

Your kisses take my breath and I feel like I'm flying up to dance among the stars.

Your fiery touch inflames me and impaled upon your shaft of light I burst in ecstasy.

I am filled with light and I am light

Once again in your arms, twin suns dancing in the sky

Finally To Dance

I knew something was wrong
Day after day the same dreary existence

I struggled to free myself but the oppressor
rarely lets go easily

There must always be a struggle

Finally I make my way out, almost like
opening my eyes for the first time I am
momentarily blinded by your light

The awe and majesty of your presence
frightens me... I run and hide in boyish
glamour.

But all truth is revealed in the bright light of
the sun. You see the woman I am, the
woman I am meant to be, and you called me
out.

No more darkness or oppression.

Only me, free at last to dance underneath
the magnificent sun.

Praises

I praise the creator of the universe, the one that set the stars in motion and led to the creation of you.

You who are full of His light and a guide on life's journey.

The Admission

You think I loved you too quickly....

If only you knew my first glance told me
that you are a King

If only you knew that when you spoke to me
I knew you were a gentle soul, intelligent,
and full of wisdom.

If only you knew that every conversation
pulled me closer while I tried to deny that
this time I really met someone that touched
me mind, body, and soul.

You think I loved you too quickly, if only
you knew I have loved you all of my life.

Let Me

My love is true, is deep, and reserved only
for the sun.

Don't let my dream end as a nightmare with
me following the moon

Let me die in a dream of my own creation
where I step away from the sun...

I step away so he can shine on those that
need him most.

The Move

"Take This Advice"

You'd better move on!

He is living his life while you sit like a sound activated toy waiting for him to call.

And when you move on he may shed a tear but he's already picked out another toy to take your place.

You don't want to move on because you say its real... it is, but real like the love a child feels for his current favorite toy. Move on because I tell you he's going to get another toy.

Move on girl, before you find yourself shut up in the toy box or broken and discarded.

You'd Better Wake Up

Wake up girl and live your life.

You won't read romance novels because they could never match the dreams in which you wrap yourself.

But girl, you'd better wake up and live your life. You sit there day-dreaming of his tender touch and soft deep voice.

You relive falling into his liquid brown eyes and surrendering to his chocolate kisses.

You waste away your hours thinking of things to do for him and to him.

You are only a footnote in his life, not a lifelong dream.

Wake up girl; you need to live your life.

Too Late

Girl you stayed too long...

You saw the warning signs and didn't go

Now here you sit with your heart broken

But why? He never promised he'd stay. It was great while you were children but now you're grown up, moved on.... And he's left you.

Childish

Sometimes I think I am still a child and not a woman. And as such, I still love like a child. Freely, fully and selfishly....

Always wanting my love within arm's reached or at least know its location...

Thinking it could not possibly be happy when not in my presence, but only because I miss my love when he's not near.

My Personal Angel

Are you my personal angel, sent down on a ray of sun to be the guardian of my heart, soul, and mind?

I thought I was lost and my soul ached from loneliness. Then you appeared like sunlight breaking through the clouds and marked my Way. Your joyous company brings me comfort and just the thought of you brightens my countenance.

My personal angel, my guardian, my sun

Waiting for My Sun to Rise

I wait in anticipation for I know the sun is almost here... the sky begins to lighten and the birds begin to sing.

I join their joyful chorus already exuberant just thinking about the sun's glorious arrival.

He calls and his voice, like the hymns of angels is so sweet in my ear. His words alone take my breath away.

Then there he is in all his magnificence. His flesh, rich chocolate brown, can barely contain his essence. His spirit shines and reaches out to me. When he kisses me, time stops. All the world fades away. I am engulfed and consumed by his light and I surrender all until there is only us, until there is only one.

The Temple

Like the veil in the holy temple your love shields me from my imperfections.

I am becoming a goddess, full of light, and bathed in light.

Bestowing the bounty of my heart to all, seeing the potential self, the true self of them all.

Stay with me my love; help me to grow in wisdom and spiritually…

Until I reach my true self and we are both gods.

What Shall I Render?

What does my angel need. He who rides on sunlight and moonbeams.

Who drinks the nectar of the gods and eats manna from heaven.

My angel, the brightest star in the heavens.

What could I possibly give him?

I am one among many that worship at his feet waiting to bathe him in love.

I Miss You

You ask me if I missed you....

If you mean did I miss

-Talking to you about everything
-Holding your hand
-Laughing at your jokes
-Hugging you
-Kissing you
-Just enjoying the nearness of you as
we become one with earth's spirit

Then yes, I missed you

Get Back

For you own protection, do not cross the line…

There is only heartbreak waiting for you.

Stay where you are so you don't see what you really mean to me

Stay where you are so you don't ask for more than I can give

Stay where you are so you can move on

For you own protection, move back from the line…

and take your heartbreak with you

Paradise Lost

I want to go back to paradise but the way is barred. I tried to bring the love that blossomed there to harsh reality.

But as with any severed blossom, it withers and dies. Withers and dies without tender caresses and kisses. Withers without sweet words.

I want to go back to paradise but the way is barred. You have closed that door that led to forever... but I still want to go back.

Unconditional Love

Can we love unconditionally?

I give you my love

Expecting you to accept and cherish it forever

Expecting you to let me stay by your side as long as I can

Expecting you to return my love

No, we cannot love unconditionally

We always expect more than is offered

Let Go, Be Free

I think I wait for you to be free

when really you are where you want to be

and it is I who needs to let you go.

The Beginning Again

Dreams of an Eternal Sun

As the sun sets I shed a tear for it is the end of one of the most beautiful days of my life. As I slept, I dreamt of a beautiful sun. I waited for dawn and when the sun rose I sang like birds praising their creator. And during that day I thought I would live forever in his beauty and warmth.

I swam in his liquid brown eyes and melted under his tender caress. All time stopped and I lost myself in his endless kisses.

But everyday must end and so here we are at sunset. I linger trying to catch the last rays of sun, knowing that nothing can stop the sun in its course.

I'll sleep one last time and lose myself in a dream where the sun rises but never sets.

Alone Again

He walks out of my life and I am in darkness. With him, my dark soul was filled with light and we burned like twin suns.

My very soul has been touched and I will never be the same again.

Only time will tell if I can continue to burn,

A single star alone in the darkness.

Too Many Questions

Don't ask questions, don't think to hard, just enjoy the illusion that you are the love of his life.

If you don't ask if he misses you when he's gone you can remain confident he wishes you were there.

Maybe he only loves you while he's here or maybe he loves you for the moment. Or maybe there's no love at all and he's just a professional.

Don't question it, aren't you having fun? Hasn't the loneliness ended?

Just accept it... and don't ask questions.

I guarantee, you won't like the answer.

It Really Doesn't Matter

If he truly loves you but will not have a future with you or if you truly are one of many...

What does it matter?

The end is the same....

Just love him while you can

Why?

Again I face the reality that maybe I really don't love anyone...

That I really just want everyone to want me, to love me, to adore me.

So why do I want to be the one, the queen, a goddess in your eyes?

Is it because of your stature, your majesty, and light?

Or is it because I just love you?

Let Me Be Your Light

He's moved away and I can barely feel his warmth. He's so far away his once tender kisses are like dappled sunlight on the cool pavement – just the illusion of warmth and comfort.

Once I felt I would be consumed in his passionate embrace but now it is gone so quickly my skin barely warms. Sunset is coming, and with it darkness and loneliness. How can I survive the long cold night knowing there will never be another sunrise?

Cone back to me my sun, even if only once, come back and consume me.

Let me store up your light for my dreams where the sun never sets.

The Queen

It's time to grow up; the Queen is not rescued from the dark castle by the handsome and powerful foreign King. As a matter of fact, she remains trapped in the castle surrounded by jesters and forced to attend to the rotting corpse of the once proud King.

Poor Queen, too strong willed to sink into insanity, instead she sinks into fantasy. A beautiful fantasy where the Sun King bathes her in love and waits for his chance to rescue her from the dark castle.

Ah, if only we could turn our fantasies into reality; time to grow up... you're not going anywhere... get back in that castle.

Cherish

I bask in his warmth and cherish each day he shines on me!

For so long I dwelt in darkness and loneliness, I held it like a shroud about me. But then the sun came, my sun, and burned away all the clouds.

And if ever tears like rain fell from my eyes, he quickly dried them all with his radiant smile.

My sun, continue to shine on me... I cherish each day you are with me.

The Force

A life force runs through us all and through out all God's creations. Every atom has its role to play and each creature has its nature to follow be it labeled wrongly good or evil.

Only man has free will to go beyond his nature, to choose to be good or evil. Other creatures just are, but we choose to be.

Is the sun evil for shining down on a thirsty land or the rain for washing away all in its path? No, God has set the universe in motion and we choose to live outside his creations.

We close our minds, bodies, and souls to that life force that connects us all. We seek to conquer instead of co-existing harmoniously. No wonder Mother Earth rails against us! And amongst ourselves we cannot recognize the bonds between us. When two people truly connect mind, body, and soul it transcends all.

We're one step closer to God...

Science

Two neutrinos dancing in the darkness

Meet
Merge

Explode in ecstasy

Lighting the world for one brief but unforgettable moment

The Confession

My secret shame, my sin
I am an enabler

I watch you get high on crack and in your shame you turn from the one you truly love

So I love you, tell you its ok, rest your head on my breast

Is it because I can love you for who you are despite your weakness and shame? Or is it because I am so desperate for even a semblance of love that I delude myself into thinking you are in love with me?

I applaud you, who gathers the strength to pry yourself from my warm embrace and cooing love sounds. But please, pity me, who must walk this land alone, always searching for love that's not drug induced.

My sin,
My secret shame,
A lonely, lonely enabler

The Escape

I need to escape this reality... rather then face the truth I continue to attempt the resurrection of a love that never was.

Sleep depravation, alcohol, gambling, bright lights, and exotic foods - that was the true substance of our love. And to seal it all, the blessing of God's beauty on our union.

In some alternate reality, we are together and as happy as we were then...

that truth I can face.

My Protector

My sun had not moved...

It was me, I turned my face from the sun

Like Mother Earth in her orbit around the sun I had moved away

But my sun, ever vigilant in his protection of me never withdrew his loving warmth.

Though I tried to fall into despair I could still feel his warmth. He called to me and I once again turn my face toward the sun.

My sun, who never moves from his protective stance, will always shine on me wherever I may be.

Wind & Water

Wind and water acting and reacting to each other

Warm currents start soft caresses that turn into passionate waves of ecstasy

Resting only for a moment before they continue their eternal dance

There Is Power In The Name

Remember your true name

Women we have freely hidden our true
selves by blindly accepting the thoughtless
name given to us at birth, then by taking on
another's name

Don't you know your true name is power?
Find yourself - look into your soul...

Remember who you were, who you are, and
who you will be

Your name as ordained by the cosmic winds
of time and patterns in the clouds, the
rhythm of the waves and sunshine

Women remember your true name and
reclaim your power!

I'm Busy

I have a thousand things to do and yet I can't seem to move from your presence.

I stand here gazing in your eyes and marveling at your majesty and glory.

My soul sings when you are near, more truly, it sings whenever I think of you.

Thank you for not sending me on my way, for letting me sit at your feet and bask in your glow.

Yes, I have a thousand things to do, and to sit in your presence is first on my list.

The Ties That Bind

Not promises but ties

Ties that bind us

Blest be the ties that bind our hearts, minds, and souls

Ties that transcend mortal reason and mortal law

Not promises made between us just ties, ties that bind

Wishing You Were Here

My day is full; I'm having fun, enjoying my family and friends

But in between it all my thoughts wander to you

What fun I'd have if you were here, hoping you're having fun and happy

Thinking of you adds just a little more brightness to my disposition

And knowing I'm another day closer to your return quickens my heart

You know the saying

"wish you were here"

The Death of What Never Was

We will never be the way things should have
been and I can't –

no I won't go back to the way things were

That moment, that woman is dead

You can mourn your loss,
the jewel you dropped in the ocean,
the flower you neglected

Mourn for all the songs left unsung, for the
light that burned out too soon

Mourn for the way things should have been
that weren't and never will be

Still Waiting

I see you waiting for things to be the way they should be…

I see so many people waiting….

Waiting, and it never happens

Waiting, while the spark of life slowly fades in her eyes

Not from the passage of time as it should be as we reach death's door

No, they are alive but not living

Waiting….

The Winding Down

You see here the winding down of a great romance - the kind only written or dreamed about but never lived

What real life love could ever endure the betrayals and miscommunications found in the novels?

And what real life love could sustain the fervor and passions of a dream?

So you see the winding down of this great romance is that we've finally reached reality

We now have a real life love that must endure betrayal, miscommunication, and yes a more realistic passion.

Passion dampened by the cares of this world but not extinguished.

You see here a great romance - the kind only real life love can bring

Please Release Me

I need you to let me go, I don't have the strength to do it on my own...

If you call me I will answer and if you come to me I will have you.

Not even my guilt can keep me away from your compassionate arms. Just the nearness of you causes my heart to beat faster and rushes the blood to...

Let me rest my weary head on your breast while you sing my praises. How smart I am, how handsome, how majestic...

I want you to call me and I want to have you. I look into your warm eyes and there is no gilt, no recrimination, only love.

No, don't let me go - I have the strength to make it if I have you...

The Winner Is...

Everybody wants to win....

I don't know why I thought you'd be any different. Only one came close to claiming that prize. That is until you came along... but what happens if I let you go there?

Will you move on? Will I be too ashamed to see you again? Or will I want you to promise to stay forever?

You've already claimed my heart and soul, and mind... must you have my body too?

Are you sure you want me all ways, always? And be my King forever?

Claim your prize then, but be prepared for the taxes!

The Galaxy

There are a billion stars in the universe...
suns each with unique characteristics.

Flora and fauna that thrive under their
own sun would perish be it mercifully quick
or agonizingly slow.

I have felt that slow painful death of one
living under the wrong sun. I used my last
breath to call out and yes like an explosion
in the darkness my world was flooded with
your light.

Your warmth constantly soothes my soul
and I am alive again when I am in your
presence. I image in my mind's eye your
exquisite physique, and the sound of my
name spoken sweetly from your luscious lips.

I can barely contain my joy, my ecstasy
when I know you will soon come to me.

My sun, created for me as I was created for
him and by him.

Where He Leads, I Will Follow

I will go wherever you lead me, I trust you will not take me where I should not go.

Such love and devotion, such trust to place my heart, my life, my very soul in your hands.

Can any mortal man bear such trust?

No wonder you flee from my presence…

I am asking you to be a god.

The Mask

When you look behind the mask and get right down to the nuts and bolts of it I'm just like everybody else...

Nothing special, same insecurities, same needs... just a mask of independence.

Loud announcements requesting solitude to avoid the reality that I am alone and not by choice. Declaring self-validation to guard my tender heart. Not wanting to love anymore because that love has never been returned.

I ventured from behind the mask and nothing has changed... so don't look for me again, you won't recognize me – I'll wear a new mask.

But underneath it all, I'm just like everybody else.

The Mask II

To stand above, to set the pace is quite a task. I was not made to stand in front.

Slowly, quietly I will fade into the background. No longer willing to expend the energy required to stay true to my reality and be labeled different, I will release it all.

I will once again become one of the masses – a sheep, not a leader. I will let the life drain from me until I am like you – wandering aimlessly, reacting but not living.

No.... I did that before and I cannot go back. I have tasted freedom and I won't be shackled again!

Call me crazy if you must but one day, you all will see the truth of my reality.

The Mask III

When you get right down to the nuts and bolts of it... I am not like everyone else...

Yes I share some of the same insecurities - that momentary lapse into humanity, my flesh once again hindering my spirit's departure from this mundane world.

And fear that you will find I am not the person you believe me to be... I've started on the path you travel but I fear you may have to leave me. I am who I am and what I am - I will not wear a mask again.

The Traveler's Prayer

We must each travel the path laid before us... and we knew inevitably there would come a time we would not walk together.

And while I wonder what your destination will be I have always known mine would be loneliness. From the beginning I have searched for completion but it seems to be an elusive dream.

Damned hope makes me look for another that completes me as you do - even though he may be a shadow. Perhaps this will suffice and my remaining journey though lonely won't be alone.

Praying our paths meet again and we can continue together until the end, and praying Tefilat Haderech.

Tefilat HaDerech- The Traveler's Prayer, is the traditional Jewish prayer for a safe journey, recited at the onset of a trip.

"...Lead us toward peace, emplace our footsteps toward peace, guide us toward peace, and make us reach our desired destination for life, gladness, and peace."

Let The Light Shine

That spark of life that is you... that bathes me in light and restore my soul.

That bit of god that you allow to shine forth - not allow, how could you possibly contain it?

Your very being exudes the power of light, your prayer has been answered - God's light shines throughout you and through you.

Shine on me, let God's light shine on me

Unspoken

Words unspoken but brought to life by actions

> *-A loving caress and soft kisses*
> *-Gentle strolls along the lake*
> *-Quiet moments dotted with sighs of contentment*

I am yours and you are mine

Those words unspoken but brought to life by actions

You are mine and I am yours

This love unspoken, brought to life by actions

For Me

He's handsome, intelligent, well spoken, and full of laughter

But does he have any sense?

Well,

He's got enough for me

Eve's Confession

(The True Story of Adam & Eve)

Oh Adam, why didn't you realize the stuff you are made of? Why didn't your power and glory shine forth? You stand before me, less than what you are.

Is it no wonder that his angelic beauty made me swoon? That his knowledge swayed me? He is pure sunlight and joy personified.

He is glorious and he offered me what I always wanted the most - to find the answers to all my questions.

Now you cannot fathom the knowledge I have... and I must move on because you can not, will not open yourself and receive.

You speak the words but your heart is closed, dark, and cold. His love pierces my very soul and I will continue my journey with him. His beauteous light will guide me and soothe my restless soul.

The Sun

I called out into the void for strength, for light, for warmth.

And the first time I saw you, saw you standing in all your majesty and power, surveying your kingdom...

I knew that you were the answer, that you would be my sun. You did not notice me – why would you? I was barely alive.

But soon I came to myself and under your glorious light I am alive again.

No more void, for you are here, my King, my strength, my light and warmth.

My sun.

Rest for The Eternal Sun

Come to me my love, let me be your shelter.

Let the King rest if only for a moment on
my ample bosom.

Let me whisper love and admiration for you
and comfort you.

I will gently caress and possess your very
soul.

Come to me my love, enter and stay forever.

Be the eternal light in my dark, dark soul.

Let me be your comfort and strength,
the giver and receiver of your love,
your companion in all ways, always.

The Plight of the Moth

I know to touch the sun is to risk being consumed in love's fiery flames

But like a moth drawn to a brightly burning candle...
so I am drawn to you my sun.

The nearness of you enflames my passion and I must touch you...

The sound of your melodious voice resonates through my body...

The very thought of you makes my heart race...

Let me come to you...

Burn away all my cares in your passionate embrace...

Let me lose myself in you until there is only one perfect moment in time when mind, soul, and flesh are one...

Let me be like the moth caught in the flame, who dies in ecstasy consumed by her sun.

Sol Invictus

"The Unconquered Sun"

I looked into the valley of my soul and found darkness…

and then,, like Moses,
I stood on the mountaintop, waiting on a word from the Lord…

Waiting for the sun to rise and light the dark shadow of my soul…

I cried out until I heard a word from the Lord…
let there be light!

And behold, there was light… and it was good

And it was you;

My Sun

Dies Natalis Solis Invicti

"The Birth of An Unconquered Sun"

I know now that I can shine even when
darkness surrounds me –
for I have once again found that spark
God gave me within myself…

that same light that I thought only you
brought forth from your soul…
Not saying that I don't need your light to
bathe me in warmth, or that I don't need
your gentle caress, or to rest in your arms…

But saying that now that you have ignited
my flames I can now light the dark recesses
of your soul…

Loving you all the more as the spark of Life
burns bright in us both…

A blessed creation as God intended it to be;
of one body, one mind, and one soul

Forever your Queen, and now; Your Sun and
you
Forever my King, and always; My Sun

All ways, Always

www.ingramcontent.com/pod-product-compliance
Lightning Source LLC
Chambersburg PA
CBHW030343310726
48979CB00001B/166

* 9 7 8 0 5 7 8 0 1 3 4 0 4 *